THE JUNIOR NOVELIZATION

THE JUNIOR NOVELIZATION

Adapted by Kiki Thorpe

Designed by Disney's Global Design Group

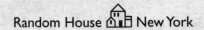

Random House New York

CHAPTER 1

A low murmur echoed through the dim interior of the Galactic Council chamber. In the packed grandstand, creatures of all shapes and sizes were whispering to one another. Alien diplomats from every planet in the galaxy had been called to the Galactic Federation headquarters on the planet Turo to witness the trial that was about to take place. Now their heads turned as a tall figure strode to the head of the room.

Suddenly a bright spotlight shone down, illuminating the gaunt blue face of the Grand Councilwoman, the leader of the Galactic Federation. Tall and slim, with a long, thin neck and dramatic antler-like lapels on her cloak, the Grand Councilwoman looked nearly as imposing as she acted. She glanced around impatiently until the room quieted down.

"Read the charges," she said to Captain Gantu, the twenty-foot-tall alien who stood at her side.

Captain Gantu lowered his mammoth head to read from the arrest report. "Dr. Jumba Jukiba, lead scientist of Galaxy Defense Industries," he boomed. "You stand before this council accused of illegal genetic experimentation."

Jumba Jukiba, a large purple alien wearing a lab coat, stood on a floating disc in the center of the council chamber. His four beady eyes shifted nervously.

"How do you plead?" the Grand Councilwoman asked Jumba.

"Not guilty!" he replied. "My experiments are only theoretical and are completely within legal boundaries."

At that moment, an armored pod floated into the chamber. In the grandstand, the alien diplomats leaned forward in their seats as the pod began to open. Metal sheaths slid aside, exposing smaller and smaller compartments until nothing was left but a single container, hovering above another disc in the center of the room.

The Grand Councilwoman eyed the scientist coldly. "We believe you actually *created* something," she said.

"Created something?" Jumba spluttered indignantly. "That would be irresponsible and unethical. I would never, ever . . ."

As he spoke, the container's cover opened, exposing its contents for all to see. Gasps echoed through the chamber as the diplomats peered at the thing inside.

". . . make more than one," Jumba finished weakly.

Crouched on the floor of a glass jar was a small, fuzzy, blue creature dressed in an orange jumpsuit. With six legs, huge ears, and a row of sharp spines running down its back, it looked like a weird combination of an insect, a bat, and a porcupine. Pressing its nose against the glass wall of the jar, it stared curiously at its alien audience. Suddenly its lips curled back in a hideous smile, revealing a mouthful of sharp yellow teeth. As the aliens watched, the creature circled its glass cage, prying at the seal with its needle-like claws. Finding no way out, it threw itself against the glass wall, hoping to break free.

"What is that monstrosity?" Captain Gantu asked.

"Monstrosity!" Jumba exclaimed. "What you see before you is the first of a new species. I call it *Experiment 626!*" The scientist's eyes shone with mad glee as he began to describe his creation. "He is bulletproof, fireproof, and can think faster than a supercomputer. He can see in the dark and move objects three thousand times his size. His only instinct ... *to destroy everything he touches*! *Hahahahahaha!*"

Jumba's wicked laughter died away, and the room fell silent. All eyes were on Experiment 626.

"So it *is* a monster," the Grand Councilwoman concluded.

"Just a little one," Jumba quickly replied.

"It is an affront to nature!" Captain Gantu exploded. "It must be destroyed!"

"Calm yourself," the Grand Councilwoman told him. "Perhaps it can be reasoned with."

She turned to the creature in the container. "Experiment 626, show us there is something inside you that is good."

The aliens held their breath. Experiment 626 tilted his head as if carefully considering the question. Then he cleared his throat.

"Meega, na la QUEESTA!" he declared.

The alien council flew into an uproar. Some aliens fainted. Others threw up. Even the Grand Councilwoman was shocked.

"So . . . *naughty!*" she said, shuddering with disgust.

"*I* didn't teach him that!" Jumba said defensively.

Captain Gantu could stand it no longer. "Place that . . . *idiot* scientist under arrest!" he shouted, pointing at Jumba.

A bell-shaped jar suddenly materialized over Jumba's floating disc, trapping him inside.

"I prefer to be called evil genius!" Jumba bellowed back to the council as he was carted away.

The Grand Councilwoman turned her attention to Experiment 626. "And as for that abomination," she said, "it is the flawed product of a deranged mind. It has no place among us. Captain Gantu, take him away."

"With pleasure," Gantu responded at once. Clenching his huge fists, he moved toward the little creature's cell.

CHAPTER 2

Blue flames spewed from the engines of the *Durgon*, the Galactic Federation's transport spaceship, as it traveled through outer space. Inside the ship's prison bay, Experiment 626 hung upside down, locked tight within an armored containment pod. Two alien guards kept their space weapons ready as they maneuvered the pod into a ceiling module and bolted it into place.

Once the pod was secured, one of the guards cautiously reached over with a syringe and took a blood sample from below the creature's ear. He handed the sample to Lieutenant Sledge, a hammer-headed alien in a blue military uniform. Sledge inserted the blood sample into two large cannons. The cannons suddenly blinked on and rotated to aim at 626. Then

Captain Gantu strolled casually over to his prisoner.

"Uncomfortable? Good. The council has banished you to exile on a distant desert asteroid. So relax, enjoy the trip, and don't get any ideas," Gantu growled. "These cannons are locked onto your genetic signature." He pointed at 626's face. "They won't shoot anyone but you."

Without warning, 626 clamped his sharp teeth down on the captain's finger.

"Ow!" Gantu bellowed, snatching his hand away. He grabbed his laser. "Why, you little . . ."

"*Ahem.*" Lieutenant Sledge cleared his throat. "May I remind the captain that he *is* on duty?"

Grumbling, Gantu holstered his weapon. "Secure the cell!" he ordered.

"Aye, Captain," Sledge said. As Captain Gantu left, the heavy metal doors slammed shut, sealing the room behind him.

Gantu strode to the bridge of the spaceship and sat down in his captain's chair. "All ahead full," he commanded. A squadron of police-escort ships switched on their navigational lights and surrounded the *Durgon*. As the spaceships moved through the starry galaxy, the captain quietly examined his bitten finger. After a moment, he sheepishly leaned over to the helmsman and asked, "Does this look infected to you?"

Back in the prison bay, Experiment 626 was dangling a gooey globule of spit from his mouth. He watched the cannons track the spit's downward path. When he sucked his saliva back up, the cannons followed it again. 626 was delighted! He continued to drool and suck his saliva.

"Quiet, you!" Lieutenant Sledge ordered.

626 sent a vile glob of spit sailing through the air. Immediately the cannons tracked the glob to the floor and let loose an explosive round of fire blasts. When the smoke cleared, Lieutenant Sledge was pressed against the door, teetering on the edge of the hole that the weapons had blasted in the floor.

626 grinned at the lieutenant and spit again.

This time the glob landed squarely on Sledge's cap. The cannons swiveled to aim at the lieutenant's head. For a split second, Lieutenant Sledge found himself staring down ten barrels of firepower. Then he ducked, leaving his cap spinning in midair. The cannons blasted the cap—and the door behind it—to smithereens.

The fire blasts echoed through the ship. On the command bridge, lights began to flash. Emergency sirens shrieked.

"He's loose on Deck C!" the first officer cried.

"Red alert! Seal off the deck!" Captain Gantu ordered.

But his order came a moment too late. In the prison bay, 626 had cracked his containment pod in two and dropped to the floor. The cannons spun and began to fire at him. Using the two halves of his broken pod as shields, 626 ran toward the closing bulkhead door. He tossed the smoldering pod halves aside and shoved his claws under the door just before it locked into place.

"Deadly force authorized. Fire on sight!"

Captain Gantu's voice blared over the ship's loudspeakers.

With a horrible grinding sound, the gears on the bulkhead door reversed as 626 wrenched it open. He darted under the door and into the passageway only to see a squadron of armed guards charging right at him!

"There he is!" the squad leader cried. The alien troopers opened fire.

Dodging the blasts, 626 ripped the cover off an air vent and ducked inside. Close on his heels, the team leader fired his laser into the duct. But Experiment 626 had already escaped through the ventilation system.

"Security to the bridge! He's in the vents!" the squad leader shouted into his radio.

On the bridge, Captain Gantu and his crew looked up at the ceiling. They could hear the creepy little creature giggling as he scurried through the vents overhead. Drawing his laser, Gantu fired a blast at the duct above him. Suddenly his expression changed from anger to alarm.

"He's headed for the power . . ."

The lights went black. The ship's engines ground to a halt.

". . . grid," Gantu finished. For a moment the ship was quiet. Then the sound of an engine broke the silence.

"What was that?" Gantu asked worriedly.

"I don't think he's on the ship anymore," a crew member replied. At that moment a red fighter ship rocketed past the window.

"Confirmed," the first officer said. "He's taken a police cruiser."

"*EEEEAAAAAAAAGHHHHH!*" 626 squealed, giggling wildly and honking the horn of the stolen ship.

But Captain Gantu wasn't going to let his prisoner escape that easily. A second later, a shower of laser blasts whistled past the cockpit of 626's cruiser. Four hundred police fighters were hot on his trail!

626 slammed on his brakes—and suddenly reversed direction! He lowered the ship's cannons and began firing as he drove straight into the center of the police formation. The police ships scattered, spinning off in every

direction as they tried to dodge 626's head-on attack.

But one ship couldn't get out of the way fast enough. It slammed into the side of 626's red cruiser.

"We got him!" the commander cried excitedly as oily smoke poured from 626's ship.

"Noogy Bay!" 626 screamed in frustration. He looked around the rattling cockpit of his destroyed vehicle. Spying an emergency handle, he smashed the safety glass and yanked the lever toward him. On the dashboard, red lights flashed.

"HYPER-DRIVE ACTIVATED," a computerized voice announced. 626 cranked the handle further. The red lights blinked frantically.

"WARNING. GUIDANCE IS NOT FUNCTIONAL," the computer said. "NAVIGATION FAILURE. DO NOT ENGAGE HYPER—"

626 slammed the handle all the way forward. The cruiser charged into hyper-drive and exploded out of the galaxy, leaving nothing behind but a massive shock wave.

Watching from the *Durgon,* Captain Gantu

and his crew braced themselves as the shock rolled toward them like a giant tidal wave. Gantu fell back into his captain's chair, pounding his fist and slumping in frustration.

Experiment 626 had escaped.

"Get me Galactic Control," Gantu said wearily.

CHAPTER 3

The doors of the control center slammed open and the Grand Councilwoman stormed into the room. "WHERE IS HE?" she roared.

"He's still in hyperspace," an alien named Grorek replied. Around them a crew of control operators worked frantically at their consoles, trying to locate the lost ship.

"Where will he exit?" asked the Grand Councilwoman.

"Calculating now," said Yeoman Aszur, a small pink alien who sat behind a control panel. A hologram showing the trajectory of 626's ship suddenly materialized in the air before them. The Grand Councilwoman watched closely as the ship flew toward a distant planet.

"Quadrant 17... Section 005... Area 51..." The hologram image magnified and zoomed in.

The ship was heading for the blue-and-green surface of . . .

"A planet called *EEE-aar-th*," Yeoman Aszur reported.

"I want an expert on this planet in here, *now*!" the Grand Councilwoman ordered. She watched the ship fly toward a large blue patch on the planet's surface.

"What is that?"

"Water," a lieutenant answered. "Most of the planet is covered in it."

The Grand Councilwoman relaxed. "He won't survive in water. His molecular density is too great." Hearing this, the relieved crew members began to cheer.

But she had spoken too soon. As the hologram image continued to zoom in, they saw that the ship was headed not for the water after all, but for a string of tiny dots in the ocean. A moment later, the Hawaiian Islands came into focus. The ship was headed straight for the island of Kauai.

The aliens groaned.

"How much time do we have?" the Grand Councilwoman asked.

"We have projected his landing at three hours, forty-two minutes," Yeoman Aszur told her.

The Grand Councilwoman made a quick decision. "We have to gas the planet."

"Hold it! Hold everything!" someone cried. The Grand Councilwoman turned. A skinny, one-eyed alien with an armload of charts was rushing toward her.

"Earth is a protected wildlife reserve," the alien said, fumbling with his charts. "We've been using it to rebuild the mosquito population, which, need I remind you, is an *endangered species*." The alien unrolled a chart showing a picture of a plump, healthy mosquito.

"Am I to assume you are the expert?" the Grand Councilwoman asked.

"Well, I don't know about *expert*. . . ." The alien chuckled modestly. But noticing the Grand Councilwoman's impatient glare, he snapped to attention. "Agent Pleakley, at your service."

"Can we not simply destroy the island?" the Grand Councilwoman asked him.

"No!" Pleakley exclaimed. "The mosquitoes' food of choice, primitive humanoid life-forms, have colonies all over that planet." Inserting a slide wheel into a plastic ViewMaster, Pleakley held the toy up to the Grand Councilwoman's eyes. The councilwoman peered at an image of a human family.

"Are they intelligent?" she asked.

"No," Pleakley answered. "But they're *very* delicate. Every time an asteroid strikes their planet, they have to begin life all over."

The Grand Coucilwoman shoved the ViewMaster back at him with a frustrated sigh. "What if our military forces just *landed* there?"

Pleakley shook his head. "Landing there would create mass mayhem and planetwide panic."

The Grand Councilwoman began to lose patience. "A quiet capture would require an understanding of 626 that we do not possess," she snapped. "Who, then, Mr. Pleakley, would you send for his extraction?"

Pleakley looked at her blankly. "Does he have a brother? A close grandmother, perhaps?"

The Grand Councilwoman narrowed her eyes thoughtfully.

In a prison cell high above the ground, Jumba Jukiba was looking at a picture of himself on the front page of a newspaper. IDIOT SCIENTIST JAILED, the headline read. Jumba growled loudly. He ripped the paper to shreds, then stuffed the pieces into his mouth.

The door to his cell suddenly slid open. The Grand Councilwoman and Pleakley stepped inside.

Jumba swallowed the last bits of newspaper and smiled smugly. "He got away?"

"I'm sure this comes as no surprise to you," the Grand Councilwoman said grimly.

"I designed this creature to be unstoppable," Jumba said with pride.

"Which is precisely why *you* must now bring him back. And to reward you, we are willing to trade your freedom for his capture," the Grand Councilwoman replied.

Jumba considered this. "626 will not come easily," he said. He thought for a moment.

"Maybe a direct hit from a plasma cannon might stun him long enough to restrain—"

"Plasma cannon granted," the Grand Councilwoman interrupted sharply. "Do we have a bargain, Dr. Jumba?"

Jumba snorted in agreement.

"B-but it's a delicate planet!" Pleakley cried. "Who's going to control him?"

"You will," said the Grand Councilwoman. Before Pleakley could reply, she turned and walked out of the room.

A crazed gleam shone in Jumba's eyes as he looked at the quivering Pleakley. "So tell me, my little one-eyed one, on what poor, pitiful, defenseless planet has my *monstrosity* been unleashed?"

CHAPTER 4

Millions of miles away from planet Turo, just off the island of Kauai, a five-year-old girl named Lilo was swimming in the ocean. Schools of colorful fish darted out of her way, and dolphins leaped into the air as she kicked up to the surface, caught her breath, then dove into the water again. A fat puffer fish swam past, carrying a peanut-butter sandwich in its mouth.

A wave lifted Lilo closer to the surface. With a little kick, she poked her head above water and expertly rode the wave to the shore. As it reached the beach, the wave curled over and Lilo tumbled onto the sand.

Lilo hopped to her feet, picked up her duffel bag, and began to run up the beach, dodging the sprawled bodies of sunbathing tourists. As she passed a large sunburned man holding a mint chocolate chip ice cream cone, she suddenly stopped. Quick as a wink, she pulled a waterproof camera out of her bag, snapped a picture of the startled man, and then darted off. The ice cream fell off the man's cone and landed in the sand with a plop.

Not far away, at a local community center, a row of teenage girls were practicing the hula. Their arms waved gracefully to a Hawaiian melody. Their hips swayed. Their fingers drew invisible pictures in the flower-scented air. The hula instructor, a large Hawaiian man, watched them and nodded approvingly.

As the dance continued, a group of little girls filed onto the stage. Dressed in ti leaf skirts, they looked like miniature versions of the older dancers. Their skirts rustled softly as they joined the hula. Their arms waved gracefully. Their hips swayed.

"One, two, three, four . . . ," the instructor counted. He stopped when he came to a gap in the line. Somebody was missing. The instructor rubbed his temples and groaned, "Aye, yae, yae."

At that moment, a soaking wet Lilo rushed

in the door and ran to the empty spot. She started to hula along with the other girls, but— *whoops!* Lilo's classmates began to slip in the puddles she'd dripped on the floor. One by one they skidded across the stage and landed in a hula heap.

"Stop! Stop!" the instructor shouted. The music came to a halt. Everyone looked at Lilo.

"Lilo, why are you all wet?" the instructor asked.

"It's sandwich day," Lilo answered.

The instructor stared at her.

"Every Thursday I take Pudge the fish a peanut-butter sandwich," she explained. "And today we were out of peanut butter so I asked my sister what to give him, and she said a *tuna* sandwich." As she spoke, Lilo became more and more agitated. "I can't give Pudge tuna!" Then Lilo asked with a whisper, "Do you know what tuna is?"

"Fish?" the hula instructor guessed.

"IT'S FISH!" Lilo shouted. "If I gave Pudge tuna, I'd be an abomination! I'm late because I had to go to the store and get peanut butter because all we have is . . . is . . ." She began to hiccup with distress. ". . . STINKING TUNA!"

The instructor put his hand on Lilo's shoulder. "Lilo, why is this so important?" he asked gently.

"Pudge controls the weather," Lilo told him matter-of-factly.

The older dancers glanced at one another. The younger girls giggled. No one knew what to make of Lilo's strange story. A little red-haired girl named Myrtle leaned in close to Lilo. "You're crazy," she said.

In a flash Lilo pounced on her, swinging her fists and scratching like a wildcat. The hula instructor grabbed Lilo, but not before she'd managed to sink her teeth into Myrtle's arm.

"I'm sorry, I'm sorry. I won't do it again!" Lilo cried as soon as he'd pulled them apart. She put her hands behind her back to show she meant it.

"Maybe we should call your sister," the instructor said.

"*No!* I'll be good. I want to dance. I practiced. I just want to dance," Lilo begged. "I practiced."

"*Eww!*" Myrtle squealed with disgust,

holding up her left arm. "She bit me!"

The hula instructor rubbed his temples and groaned again.

A half hour later, Lilo was sitting cross-legged on the front porch of the hula school, waiting for the rest of the class to finish their lesson. Behind her, the door of the studio opened and the other little girls filed out, flouncing past Lilo as if she weren't there. The hula instructor came out and knelt down next to Lilo.

"I called your sister," he told her. "She said to wait for her here on the porch."

Lilo nodded and turned away. On the crushed-seashell path outside the building, the other girls were holding pretty dolls and chattering happily together. Lilo watched them enviously.

The girls were gathered around Myrtle, examining Lilo's teeth marks on her arm. "Does this look infected to you?" Myrtle asked one of the girls. Myrtle looked at Lilo. "You better not have rabies," she said.

"If you have rabies, the dog catcher will have

to cut your head off," another girl chimed in.

Lilo ignored this remark. "Are you gonna play dolls?" she asked hopefully.

The girls tried to hide their dolls behind their backs. They didn't want to play with Lilo. "You don't have a doll," Myrtle pointed out.

Lilo reached into her duffel bag and pulled out a floppy rag doll with buttons for eyes and a lopsided smile. "This is Scrump," she said.

The girls drew back in horror. Scrump was the ugliest doll they'd ever seen.

Lilo looked proudly at her toy. "I made her," she said. "But her head is too big, so I pretend a bug laid eggs in her ears and she is upset because she only has a few more days . . ."

But when she looked up, the other girls were gone. Lilo's eyes filled with tears. Nobody ever wanted to be her friend! She threw Scrump to the ground and ran away.

A moment later she was back. She picked Scrump up and dusted her off. Cradling her doll like a baby, Lilo sadly walked home.

CHAPTER 5

A little while later, a pretty young Hawaiian woman stood on the steps of the hula school. It was Nani, Lilo's older sister. She'd come to pick up Lilo.

"Lilo?" she said, looking around the empty porch. "Lilo?" She peered in the windows of the school. No one was inside.

"Oh, no," Nani said with a sigh. She turned on her heel and sprinted off in search of her sister.

"You'd better be home, Lilo," Nani said, panting, racing down the dirt roads that led to their home. As she rounded a corner, a large blue car suddenly pulled out in front of her. The car skidded to a stop.

"Hey! Watch where you're going, stupid head!" Nani shouted at the driver. She kicked the front of the car, then dashed off in a huff.

Nani bounded up the front steps to their house—only to find that the door was locked! Strains of Elvis Presley music drifted out through the windows. Nani banged on the wooden door. "Lilo? Open the door!" she shouted.

"Go away," Lilo replied.

Dropping to all fours, Nani stuck her head through the dog door and looked into the living room. Lilo lay on the floor, gazing at the ceiling. Music blared from a record player next to her.

Nani scowled. "Lilo, we don't have time for this. The social worker is gonna be here any minute!" Without looking at her sister, Lilo slowly lifted her arm and turned up the volume on the record player.

Nani squeezed her arm through the dog door and flipped the lock. But the door still wouldn't budge. Lilo had nailed it shut!

"Argggh!" Nani groaned. She grabbed the hammer Lilo had left near the door and frantically began to pry out the nails. "You are *so* finished when I get in there," she growled at her little sister. "I'm gonna stuff you in the

blender, push Puree, then bake you into a pie and feed it to the social worker. And when he says, 'Mmm, this is great. What's your secret?' I'm gonna say—"

Suddenly Nani was pulled out of the doorway by her feet. She looked up. A huge man in dark sunglasses towered over her.

"—love and nurturing!" she said quickly. She scrambled to her feet and held out her hand. "Hi! You must be the—" Nani stopped abruptly, realizing she was still holding the hammer.

"The *stupid head*," the man finished for her. Nani looked behind him at the blue car parked in the driveway. There was a big dent in the front fender where Nani had kicked it.

"Oh!" Nani gasped. "Oh, I'm *really* sorry. I can pay for that."

"It's a rental," the man said gruffly. "Are you the guardian in question?"

"Yes! I'm Nani. Nice to meet you, Mr. . . . ."

"Bubbles," the large man muttered sheepishly. "Are you going to invite me in, Nani?"

"Right. Uh . . . this way," said Nani. She led Mr. Bubbles over the porch railing and through the dense bushes around the house, praying that the back door would be unlocked. It wasn't.

"Uh, wait here," she told the giant social worker.

Mr. Bubbles waited by the back door as Nani trudged off around the house. Suddenly—*crash!*—he heard a window breaking. Footsteps clomped through the house, and the Elvis music abruptly scratched off. A second later, Nani flung open the back door, smiling breathlessly. "So, lemonade?" she offered.

Mr. Bubbles strode past her and looked around. "Do you often leave your sister home alone?" he asked as he walked toward the kitchen.

"No. Never!" Nani said, hurrying after him. "Well, except for just now. I had to run to the store to get some—" Nani broke off in horror. The kitchen looked like a meteorite had struck it. Spilled food and open jars littered the counters. Pots filled with stewy glop bubbled over on the stove. Nani raced to turn off the burners.

Mr. Bubbles raised his eyebrows. "You left the stove on while you were out?"

"Low heat. Just a simmer." Nani lifted the lid of one of the pots and screamed. She slammed down the lid before the social worker could see what was inside.

"I found that this morning," Lilo piped up from behind them.

"Lilo! There you are, Honeyface!" Nani exclaimed. "This is Mr. . . . Bubbles."

Mr. Bubbles held his giant hand out for Lilo to shake. Lilo stared. The letters *C-O-B-R-A* were tattooed across his knuckles.

"Your knuckles say *Cobra*," Lilo said. Mr. Bubbles cracked his knuckles as he bent down to get a closer look at Lilo. "Cobra Bubbles, you don't look like a social worker," she continued.

Cobra waited for a moment. "We're getting off the subject. Let's talk about you," he said quickly. "Are you happy?"

Lilo beamed a phony smile and began to recite the speech she and Nani had practiced. "I eat four food groups and only watch the church channel and take long naps . . ."

Behind Cobra Bubbles' back, Nani shook her fist triumphantly. But Lilo misunderstood.

"... and get disciplined," she said.

"Disciplined?" Cobra Bubbles asked. Nani's joy turned to panic. She waved her hands, signaling Lilo to stop. Again, Lilo misinterpreted.

"Yeah. Sometimes five times a day!" she said cheerfully. "With bricks."

"Bricks?"

"Uh-huh. In a pillowcase."

Nani couldn't stand it any longer. "Okay!" she cried, pushing Lilo toward the living room. "That's enough sugar for you!" She turned to their guest with a nervous laugh. "The other social workers just thought she was a scream."

But Cobra Bubbles wasn't laughing. "Let me illuminate to you the precarious situation in which you have found yourself," he said sternly. "I am the one they call when things go wrong." He looked around the disastrous kitchen. "And things have indeed gone wrong."

Cobra strode into the living room, leaned down, and handed his business card to Lilo. "Call me next time you're left here alone," he said.

He turned back to Nani. "In case you're

wondering, this did *not* go well," he said with a scowl. With an effortless yank, he wrenched the front door open, ripping the nails out of the door frame. "You have three days to change my mind."

CHAPTER 6

When Cobra Bubbles was gone, Nani ran after Lilo. "Why didn't you wait at the school?" she cried. "You were supposed to wait there!"

Lilo tried to wriggle away, but her older sister held her tight.

"Do you not understand? Do you want to be taken away?" Lilo turned her head away from her sister. Tears welled up in her eyes. "Answer me!" Nani demanded.

"No!" said Lilo.

"No, you don't understand?" asked Nani.

"*Nooooooo!*" Lilo shouted. Confused and upset, she flopped facedown on the floor.

Nani gave up. "You are *such* a pain," she said tiredly.

Lilo jumped up from the floor. "So why don't you sell me and buy a rabbit instead!" she cried. She ran up the stairs to her room. Nani followed.

"At least a rabbit would behave better than you!" Nani cried.

"Go ahead! Then you'll be happy because it will be *smarter* than me, too!" Lilo yelled.

"And *quieter,*" Nani added.

"YOU'LL LIKE IT 'CAUSE IT'S STINKY LIKE YOU!" Lilo shot back. She slammed her bedroom door.

"GO TO YOUR ROOM!" Nani shouted.

Lilo's door flew open. "I'M ALREADY IN MY ROOM!" she cried. She slammed the door again.

Nani went to the sofa, picked up a pillow, and placed it over her face. *"Aaaaaaaaaah!"* she screamed.

Upstairs, Lilo was screaming into a pillow on her bed. *"Aaaaaaaaaaah!"*

Later that night, Lilo was sitting in bed when there was a gentle knock on her door.

"Hey," Nani said, poking her head into the

room. She opened the door. "I brought you some pizza in case you were hungry."

"We're a broken family, aren't we?" Lilo said sadly.

Nani came and knelt by Lilo's bed. "No . . . maybe a little . . . maybe a lot," she said. "I shouldn't have yelled at you."

"We're sisters, it's our job," Lilo answered. She looked at her older sister. "I like you better as a sister than a mom."

"Yeah?"

"And you like me better as a sister than a rabbit, right?" Tears flooded Lilo's big, brown eyes.

Nani sat on the bed and rocked the little girl in her arms. "Oh, yes. Yes, I do," she told her, gently consoling Lilo.

"I hit Myrtle Edmonds today," Lilo said suddenly.

Nani frowned. "You hit her?"

"Before I bit her," Lilo admitted.

"You *bit* her? Lilo you shouldn't—" Nani started to scold.

"People treat me different," Lilo said sadly.

"They just don't know what to say," Nani said, trying to make her sister feel better. She knew things had been tough for Lilo since their parents died. It had been hard for both of them. "Tell you what," she decided. "If you promise not to fight anymore, I promise not to yell at you—except on special occasions."

"Tuesdays and bank holidays would be good," Lilo said.

"Yeah?" Nani smiled. "Would that be good?" She grabbed Lilo and tickled her. They both laughed.

"Oh!" Lilo cried, suddenly remembering. "My camera is full again!" She handed Nani her little camera. They both looked at Lilo's photo collection. On the wall over her bed, Lilo had pinned dozens of snapshots of overweight tourists. Lilo sighed. "Aren't they beautiful?" she said.

Just then the hula-girl lamp beside Lilo's bed flickered and went out. Outside the window, a bright, burning object streaked through the sky. The clouds glowed like lanterns as it passed. Seconds later, Nani and Lilo saw the light from a big explosion several miles away.

"A falling star!" Lilo cried. "I call it!" She began to shove Nani out of her room. "Get out! Get out! I have to make a wish!"

But Nani couldn't resist the chance to tease her sister. "Oh, no!" she cried, grabbing her stomach. "Gravity is increasing on me!" She started to fall backward onto Lilo.

"NO, IT'S NOT!" Lilo roared, pushing her sister out the door.

"It is too, Lilo. The same thing happened yesterday," Nani said calmly. She fell back flat on the floor, pinning Lilo underneath her.

"You rotten sister! Your butt is crushing me!" Lilo yelped. Finally she squirmed free, ran into her room, and slammed the door.

Nani sat up and opened Lilo's door a crack. Lilo was kneeling beside her bed with her eyes closed. Her hands were clasped tightly together.

"It's me again. I need someone to be my friend," Lilo was saying. "Someone who won't run away. Maybe send me an angel . . ."

Nani's shoulders sagged with dismay. She'd had no idea her sister was so lonely.

"... the nicest angel you have," Lilo finished her prayer.

At that moment on another part of the island, Experiment 626 was climbing out of the huge crater created when his burning ship had crashed into the ground. He looked at the lush tropical forest around him and smiled wickedly. His yellow teeth gleamed in the darkness.

"Poodja cha-bagga, oon cheeky!" he called out. Cackling with delight, he scampered off through the trees.

CHAPTER 7

Experiment 626 stood in the middle of a dark, deserted road. His huge ears were pricked up, listening for the slightest sound.

Suddenly something fell out of the sky and landed on the ground next to him. In a flash, 626 drew his laser and vaporized the object. Another one fell, landing right on his head. He pointed his weapon upward and fired into the sky. But he was no match for the raindrops that came pelting down. A second later, 626 was soaked by a sudden downpour. He hissed miserably.

Just then, two strong beams of light caught 626 in their glare. Through the pouring rain, the outline of a tractor trailer was barely visible. 626 aimed his laser at the lights and . . .

POW! A giant set of tires mowed him down. *POW! POW! POW!* One by one, a convoy of large trucks rolled over the little alien, ripping his orange jumpsuit to shreds. Their tires popped as they hit the sharp spikes on his back. The trucks skidded to a stop. The drivers leaped out.

"What did we hit?" the first driver asked.

They shined their flashlights up under the wheels of the last truck. "There it is! It stayed jammed up under the fender!" said one of the men.

At that moment one of Experiment 626's sharply clawed paws fell into view. The drivers jumped back in fright.

"We better call somebody," the first driver said.

The next morning, when 626 came to, he was lying on the floor of a kennel in an animal rescue center. In the far corner of the cage, a group of dogs were huddled together, nervously watching him. 626 automatically reached for his laser—but both his laser and his uniform were gone!

"Inja, koata-nabba!" the little alien shouted.

But the dogs just whined and huddled closer together. Disgusted, 626 grabbed the kennel bars, bent them open, and walked out.

In the rescue center's main office, Nani and Lilo were talking with the woman in charge of animal adoptions.

"We're looking for something that can defend itself," Nani explained to the rescue woman. "Something . . . sturdy."

"Like a lobster," Lilo suggested.

"Lilo, you lolo. Do we have a lobster door? No, we have a dog door. We're getting a dog," Nani said.

No one noticed the strange blue creature clinging to the ceiling. 626 scurried past them on a wooden beam above the reception area and slipped out the front door.

But the instant he set foot outside, a scorching energy blast singed the tips of his blue fur. 626 ducked behind a boulder as more shots rained around him.

"Ha, ha! So nice to see your pretty face again!" a familiar voice chuckled.

"Jumba!" 626 cried.

In a flash, 626 ducked through the screen door of the rescue center. He scuttled across the ceiling and back into the kennel.

In the office, the rescue center woman opened the door to the kennel and motioned for Lilo to come through.

"Go," Nani told her little sister. "Pick someone out."

Lilo stepped hesitantly into the kennel. "Hello?" she said, looking around. "Hello?"

But she didn't see a single animal. All the terrified dogs were clinging to the tops of their cages—well out of Experiment 626's way.

Hidden in the shadows, 626 watched Lilo. Just then a poster on the wall caught his eye. In the picture, a girl and her dog were happily hugging. 626 looked thoughtfully at the poster. It gave him an idea! He scrunched his middle two appendages into his belly until they were completely hidden. He folded his antennae and the thorny spikes on his back into his fur. Then he got down on all fours. Experiment 626 looked just like a dog. Sort of.

When Lilo turned around, he was sitting

right in front of her. Lilo looked at him with surprise.

"Hi," she said.

626 stood up. "H-h-h-h-hi," he said. He grabbed Lilo and hugged her, just like the dog in the poster.

Lilo's eyes opened wide. "Wow!" she exclaimed. He was the most amazing dog she'd ever seen! With 626 at her side, Lilo walked back into the main office.

But when Nani and the rescue woman saw the horrible blue creature, they leaped backward. Nani grabbed Lilo and jumped onto a chair. The rescue woman grabbed 626.

"What *is* that thing?" Nani asked.

"A dog, I think," the woman answered. "But it was dead this morning."

Nani's eyebrows lifted. "It was dead this morning?"

"We thought it was dead. It was hit by a truck," the woman explained.

"I like him. Come here, boy," Lilo said.

"Wouldn't you like a different dog?" Nani's voice rose in panic as 626 tugged free of the rescue woman and walked toward them. He crawled up Nani's leg and grabbed Lilo, dragging them both to the floor.

"We have better dogs," the rescue woman told them.

"Not better than him! He can talk! Say hello!" Lilo commanded.

"Hhhhhh-hhhell—" 626 started to say.

"Dogs can't talk, dear," said the rescue woman. 626 abruptly shut his mouth.

"Does it have to be *this* dog?" Nani asked.

Lilo looked closely at the creature as 626 stuck his tongue into his nose. "Yes," she said. "He's good. I can tell."

The rescue woman set to work filling out the adoption form. "You'll have to think of a name for him," she told Lilo.

The little girl thought for a moment. "His name is . . . Stitch."

The woman looked confused. "That's not a real name . . . ," she started. But then she saw Nani shaking her head. ". . . in Iceland," she finished. "But here it's a good name." She nodded. "Stitch it is," the woman said as she finished the adoption form. "There's a two-dollar license fee."

As Nani reached into her pocket for the money, Lilo exclaimed, "*I* want to buy him!" She turned to her older sister. "Can I borrow two dollars?"

Nani handed the two dollars to Lilo. Lilo handed it back to Nani, who gave it to the rescue woman. The woman stamped the document and handed a pink receipt to Lilo.

"He's all yours," she said.

CHAPTER 8

Meanwhile, on a hillside far above the animal shelter, Jumba was watching them through the infrared scope of his plasma cannon.

A second later, Stitch stepped out onto the porch of the shelter. Jumba aimed his cannon. A targeting laser dot danced across Stitch's body. Stitch glanced at the glowing red dot but didn't move.

"Why don't you run?" Jumba wondered aloud. He tightened his finger on the trigger.

Stitch decided to test Jumba. He let out a doglike bark. "I'm coming, I'm coming," Lilo said. She dashed over and threw her arms around her new pet. The laser dot glowed on Lilo's back.

"Stop!" Pleakley cried, slapping Jumba's cannon away in the nick of time. The blast fired harmlessly into the sky.

Jumba grabbed Pleakley and tossed him out of the way. "Don't worry," Jumba growled. "I won't hit her!" He started to re-aim, but Pleakley popped up and stuck his finger in the barrel of the cannon.

"No!" Pleakley said. "That girl is part of the mosquito food chain." He whipped out the plastic ViewMaster and stuck it in front of Jumba's face. "Here. Educate yourself."

Jumba stared into the ViewMaster, then looked back at Stitch. His eyes narrowed angrily. "Using a little girl for a shield. This is low, even for you."

Stitch grinned at Jumba and waved his furry bottom in the air.

Jumba was furious. "I will tear him apart with all both my bare hands!" he roared. He stood up and began to march toward the animal shelter.

Seeing Jumba approaching, Stitch barked loudly. Nani, Lilo, and the rescue woman all turned to look—just as Pleakley tackled Jumba and pulled him back into the bushes.

"Have you lost your mind?" Pleakley

gasped. "You can't *shoot* and you can't be *seen*. Look at you. You look like a monster. We have to blend in!"

On the porch, Stitch smiled triumphantly. But his smirk came a moment too soon. "Bad dog, barking at nothing," the rescue woman scolded. She aimed a squirt bottle full of water at him and gave him a good soaking. Stitch grimaced—he hated water.

Later that day, Jumba and Pleakley watched from their hiding place in the bushes as Nani knelt down next to Lilo and handed her a few dollars. "Okay, I gotta get to work. Stick around town and stay out of the roads," she instructed. "I'll meet you at one." She blew a raspberry kiss on Lilo's cheek. Lilo giggled.

Stitch paid no attention to Lilo or Nani. He was fascinated by the television displays in the electronics store. He smiled with delight as he watched an old black-and-white monster movie. He even began to imitate the monster by stomping around on the sidewalk.

Just then the tinkle of a bicycle bell rang through the warm air. Across the street, the girls from Lilo's hula class were sitting on their tricycles, waiting to cross the road.

"My friends!" Lilo cried happily. She waved and sprinted over to them.

"What do *you* want?" Myrtle sneered.

"I'm sorry I bit you," Lilo said sincerely. "And pulled your hair. And punched you in the face."

"Apology *not* accepted," Myrtle snapped. "Now get out of my way before I run you over."

Stitch walked up and sat down at Lilo's side. Myrtle screamed in fright.

"I got a new dog," Lilo proudly told the girls. "His name is Stitch."

The girls wrinkled their noses. "That . . . is the ugliest thing I have ever saw," Myrtle said as Stitch crept closer and began to sniff at her trike. Suddenly he dumped Myrtle off and leaped onto the seat. Grabbing Lilo, he sped off down the street.

"Oh, great!" Pleakley exclaimed in frustration. "His destructive programming is taking effect," Jumba observed. "He will be irresistibly drawn to large cities, where he will back up sewers, reverse street signs, and steal everyone's left shoe."

And indeed, Stitch frantically pedaled the stolen trike all over the island. But all he could find were peaceful, sandy beaches and rocky seaside cliffs—there was no large city in sight! When they came to yet another deserted beach, Stitch threw up his hands in despair.

Lilo sighed and looked around happily. "It's nice to be on an island with no large cities," she said. Hearing this, Stitch keeled over in a fit of frustration.

Lilo looked at him. "Are you okay?"

CHAPTER 9

That day, Lilo took Stitch with her everywhere. She was delighted to have a dog to play with—except that Stitch wasn't acting much like a dog.

Lilo's first mission was to teach her new pet how to fetch. Armed with a squirt bottle, she threw a stick again and again. "Fetch!" she cried, squirting Stitch with water every time he disobeyed her order. To Lilo's astonishment, Stitch snatched the bottle out of her hand and tossed it away. By the end of the lesson, Lilo was the only one who had done any fetching.

Stitch's normally bad temper was becoming worse by the minute. At lunchtime, he tried to steal Lilo's food, but Nani swatted his paw away. Stitch was about to deliver a powerful smack in return . . . when a whistle suddenly caught his attention. Across the street, Jumba smiled and waved his plasma cannon. Stitch gritted his teeth and put down his fist. He couldn't harm the humans—they were his protection from Jumba!

Stitch was restless, and desperate to find someplace where he could really cause trouble. While Lilo was collecting seashells, a volleyball came flying through the air and hit Stitch on the head. Stitch was annoyed! He picked up the ball and threw it with all his might back to the volleyball player. The player fell backward onto the sand. He shook his head and gave Stitch an angry stare. Stitch ran back over to Lilo for protection.

Later that afternoon, Lilo and Stitch were sitting on the curb, eating shave ice, when a dog passed by. The dog sidled over and gave Stitch a friendly sniff. Before Lilo could stop him, her pet dumped his sticky ice cone right on the dog's head.

As Lilo dragged Stitch away, his face

suddenly broke into a grin. Could it be? A spaceship was sitting right in the middle of the sidewalk! Stitch squealed with joy and scrambled into the driver's seat. Lilo smiled and dropped a quarter into the metal box next to the ship. The ship blinked on and began to rock Stitch gently back and forth. It was only a kiddie ride. He did the only thing left to do. He threw a temper tantrum.

Jumba watched him and chuckled. "When you are ready to give up, just let us know!"

CHAPTER 10

A fearsome war cry split the night air. On a wooden stage, a young Hawaiian man twirled two flaming torches. Firelight flickered across the awed faces of sunburned tourists as they watched the dancer's daring performance.

The fire dancer suddenly blew a column of flame into the sky. The audience gasped and began to applaud. The dancer took a bow. Suddenly part of the thatched roof fell at his feet. He'd accidentally set fire to the roof above the stage!

Sitting at a nearby table, Stitch giggled wickedly as he watched the dancer try to stomp out the flames. In the seat next to him, Lilo was busily drawing with her crayons. She finished her drawing and held it up. It was a picture of Stitch, three-quarters colored in with a red crayon.

Lilo pointed at the drawing. "This is you," she said to Stitch. "This is your badness level. It's unusually high for someone your size." She narrowed her eyes at him. "We need to fix that."

At that moment, Nani, dressed in a waitress's uniform, whisked past their table, carrying a tray piled high with empty plates. She stopped when she saw Stitch. "Aye, yae, yae. Lilo, your dog cannot sit at the table," she scolded.

"Stitch is troubled. He needs desserts," Lilo told her seriously.

Nani scooped up Lilo's dinner plate and frowned. "You didn't even eat your sweet potato."

"Desserts!" Lilo replied. Nani sighed and disappeared through the doors to the kitchen.

Just then David, the fire dancer, shuffled by. His unhappy face was black with soot.

"David! I got a new dog!" Lilo called to him.

David flinched when he saw Stitch. "Whoa. You sure it's a dog?"

"Uh-huh." Lilo nodded. "He used to be a collie before he got run over."

Nani returned from the kitchen with a piece of coconut cake. Lilo's eyes lit up. But before she could take a single bite, Stitch snatched the cake and stuffed it in his mouth. A second later, he gagged and spit it out again.

Meanwhile, David was trying to work up the courage to ask Nani out on a date. "Listen," he said, running a hand through his hair. "I was wondering . . . if you're not doing anything this—"

Nani cut him off. "David, I told you. I can't. I—" She glanced over at Lilo and Stitch, then lowered her voice. "I've got a lot to deal with right now."

David lowered his voice, too. "I just figured you might need some time—"

"Look, I gotta go. The kid at table three is throwing poi again. Maybe some other time, okay?" Nani hurried off to another table. David sadly watched her leave.

"Don't worry," Lilo told him sympathetically. "She likes your butt and fancy hair. I know, I read her diary."

David's brow wrinkled. "She thinks it's fancy?"

Meanwhile, Stitch had slipped away from the table, following a delicious smell. His nose led him to a tourist's purse. He reached in, pulled out some weird-looking alien food, and began to gobble it down.

Suddenly a large purple hand shot out and grabbed him. Stitch looked up. It was Jumba! Wearing a tiny hat, a fake mustache, and a huge Hawaiian shirt, the big purple alien was dressed up to look like a tourist. Pleakley sat next to him, disguised in a wig and a flowered dress.

"Aha! Look what I find!" Jumba chuckled. "Get restraints," he told Pleakley.

Pleakley fumbled with a pair of handcuffs. But he wasn't fast enough. Suddenly Stitch opened his mouth—and swallowed Pleakley's entire head! The one-eyed alien screamed.

Nani looked up and gasped in horror at the sight of her customer's head in Stitch's mouth. "Shoo!" she screamed at Stitch. She hurried over to the table and began to pummel Stitch with her fists. Desperate, she grabbed a pitcher of iced tea and dumped it over his head.

Sputtering, Stitch spit out Pleakley's head. Jumba let go of Stitch, who scurried back to Lilo's table. From a safe distance, Stitch tauntingly waved the food he'd swiped. Jumba clenched his fists angrily.

Meanwhile, Nani was fussing over the gasping Pleakley. "Ah!" she cried, looking at his large one-eyed head. "Your head looks swollen!"

"Actually, she's just ugly," Jumba told her.

Unfortunately, the commotion had attracted the restaurant manager's attention. "Nani, is that your dog?" he asked. Before Nani could explain, the manager said, "This is not working out."

"But . . . ," Nani started, making one last attempt to work things out.

The manager sternly crossed his arms. Sadly, Nani collected Lilo and Stitch. Together they walked home.

CHAPTER 11

"**D**id you lose your job because of Stitch and me?" Lilo asked Nani as they walked up the steps of their home.

"Nah," Nani responded. "The manager's a vampire and he wanted me to join his legion of the undead."

"I knew it!" Lilo said.

"This is a great home!" Lilo said proudly, leading Stitch through the front door. "You'll like it a lot." In reply, Stitch snarled and shoved Lilo to ground. He grabbed a pillow from the couch and shredded it to pieces.

"What is the matter with you?" Nani exclaimed, taking away what was left of the pillow.

"Meega, na la QUEESTA!"

ROARRR!

"This is Scrump. I made her,
but her head is too big."

"Leave me alone."

"Cobra Bubbles? You don't look
like a social worker."

"I need someone to be my friend. Someone who
won't run away. Maybe send me an angel—
the nicest angel you have."

"His name is Stitch."

"Heh, heh! When you are ready to give up, just let us know."

"This is you. This is your badness level.
It's unusually high for someone your size.
We need to fix that."

"'Ohana means family. Family means nobody gets
left behind, but if you want to leave, you can."

"You're alive!"

"Hello, Cobra Bubbles?
Aliens are attacking my house!"

Vroom!

**"This is Gantu. Connect me to
the Grand Councilwoman."**

"I bought Stitch at the shelter. I paid
two dollars for him—see this stamp?"

"Aloha!"

"Be careful of the little angel!" Lilo cried. Suddenly Stitch curled up and rolled across the floor like a blue beach ball. Nani watched his strange locomotion with concern.

"It's not an angel," she said. "I don't even think it's a dog. He's creepy, Lilo. I won't sleep knowing he's loose in the house."

"You're loose in the house all the time and I sleep just fine," Lilo snapped back.

Meanwhile, in the kitchen, Stitch had opened all the drawers and dumped their contents onto the floor. Forks, spoons, and knives were scattered across the linoleum. When Lilo and Nani entered, he was wrestling with a whirring blender. Nani rushed over and pulled the blender away.

"Look at him, Lilo. He's obviously mutated from something else. We have to take him back," she said. She began to drag Stitch toward the door. He screamed with anger.

Lilo wasn't about to let her sister take her only friend away. "He was an orphan and we adopted him!" she cried. "What about *ohana*?"

"He hasn't been here that long!" her sister

answered, continuing to tug at Stitch.

"Neither have I!" Lilo shouted. "Dad said *'ohana* means family!"

To Stitch's surprise, Nani stopped.

"*'Ohana* means family," Lilo repeated. "Family means nobody . . ."

Nani sighed. "Nobody gets left behind," she recited with her sister.

"Or?" asked Lilo.

"Or forgotten. I know, I know. I hate it when you use *'ohana* against me," Nani said, letting go of Stitch. He jumped up and scampered away through the house. Lilo eagerly followed him.

Upstairs, Stitch kicked open the door to Lilo's room.

"This is my room," Lilo told him. "And this is your bed," she said, pointing to a pineapple crate she'd fixed up with a pillow and blanket. She held up Scrump and a baby bottle. "This is your dolly and bottle." Lilo shook the bottle. "See? It doesn't spill. I filled it with coffee."

Stitch grabbed the bottle, shoved Lilo to the floor, and jumped onto her big, fluffy bed.

"Hey! That's mine!" Lilo cried, climbing

back onto her bed. "Down!"

Stitch threw the pillow over her head. Suddenly he noticed a photograph that had been hidden beneath the pillow. He picked it up.

"BE CAREFUL OF THAT!" Lilo shouted. She yanked the photo out of his hands. "You don't touch this," she warned, sliding the picture back into its hiding place. "Don't ever touch it," she repeated.

But Stitch's destructive instincts were taking over. He ran around Lilo's room, tearing up everything he could find, snarling and slobbering like a rabid dog.

Lilo grabbed a lei and threw it around his neck. Stitch immediately quieted down. Leis apparently had an odd calming effect on the little alien.

"There." Lilo sighed. "You know, you wreck everything you touch. Why not try and *make* something for a change?"

Stitch thought about this. Moments later, he'd built a miniature city out of objects in Lilo's room.

"Wow!" Lilo said admiringly. "San Francisco!"

Then without warning, Stitch stormed through the city, growling like Godzilla and knocking it to the ground. He was acting just like the monster in the movie he had seen earlier that afternoon!

Lilo frowned. "No more caffeine for you."

From his hilltop hiding place, Jumba watched Lilo and Stitch through his quadnoculars, a pair of giant binoculars specially built for his four eyes.

"Heh, heh," he chuckled. "This little girl is wasting her time. 626 cannot be taught to ignore its destructive programming."

CHAPTER 12

Later that night, after Lilo was asleep, Stitch wandered through her room, drinking a can of soda. He belched, crumpled the can against his forehead, and tossed it on the floor. Standing amid the rubble of his model city, Stitch suddenly paused, unsure of what to do next.

Up on the hillside, Jumba continued to observe him through the quadnoculars. "This is interesting," he remarked.

"What?" asked Pleakley.

"626 was designed to be a monster, but now he has nothing to destroy," Jumba explained. "You see, I never gave him a greater purpose. What must it be like to have nothing, not even memories to visit in the middle of the night?" he wondered aloud.

In Lilo's bedroom, Stitch was pulling book

after book off her bookshelf, flipping through the pages and tearing out the pictures he liked. Opening a picture book with a yellow duck on the cover, he stopped, suddenly curious. He carried the book over to Lilo's bed and shook her awake.

Lilo looked at the book. "That's *The Ugly Duckling,*" she said sleepily. "See?" She pointed to a picture of a small, sad-looking duck. The little duck was saying, "I'm lost!"

"He's sad because he is all alone and nobody wants him," Lilo explained. She pointed to another picture. "But on this page his family hears him crying and they find him. Then the ugly duckling is happy because he knows where he belongs."

Stitch stared at the pictures for a long time. Then he grabbed the book and crawled into his pineapple-crate bed.

"Want to listen to the King?" Lilo asked him. She held up a record. "You look like an Elvis fan."

Early the next morning, Lilo and Stitch crept into the bedroom where Nani lay fast asleep. "Nani," Lilo called. Nani opened her eyes. Lilo and Stitch were standing at the foot of her bed, holding a small record player.

"Look," said Lilo. She turned on the record player and placed one of Stitch's claws on the spinning record. Then Lilo opened Stitch's mouth. Music blared out. When Lilo closed his mouth, the music abruptly stopped.

Nani was astonished.

Just then a loud knock startled her. She jumped out of bed and went to answer the front door.

Cobra Bubbles was standing on the doorstep. "Heard you lost your job," he said.

Nani quickly tried to cover. "Well, actually I just quit that job because, you know, the hours were not conducive to the challenges of raising a child."

Suddenly Stitch ran to the doorway and hurled a book at Cobra, whacking him squarely in the head.

Nani gasped. "I am so sorry about that!"

"What is that thing?" asked Cobra.

"That's my puppy!" Lilo announced.

"Really?" Cobra said, frowning at Nani. "Thus far you have been adrift in the sheltered harbor of my patience. But I cannot ignore you being jobless. Do I make myself clear?"

Nani gulped. "Perfectly."

He turned to Lilo. "And the next time I see this dog, I expect it to be a model citizen. *Capisce?*"

"Uh, yes." Lilo said even though she wasn't quite sure what the word meant.

"New job. Model citizen. Good day." Cobra put his sunglasses back on. As he walked away, one of the lenses popped out.

CHAPTER 13

Nani, Stitch, and Lilo set out to find Nani a new job. Their first stop was Mrs. Hasagawa's produce market.

"I'm here to answer your newspaper ad," Nani said to the elderly woman who owned the store.

Mrs. Hasagawa, who was somewhat hard of hearing, looked up from the fruit she was washing. "I CAN'T TALK NOW, DEAR," she said. "I'M WAITING FOR SOMEONE TO ANSWER MY AD."

Meanwhile, Lilo was trying to turn her pet into a model citizen—Lilo style.

"Elvis Presley was a model citizen," she informed Stitch. She held up an album cover and pointed to the photo of Elvis. "I've compiled a list of his traits for you to practice.

Number one is dancing." She handed Stitch a ti leaf skirt. "Now, follow my lead."

Moments later, Lilo and the newly dressed Stitch were hula dancing through the store, past bins full of pineapples and bananas. Faster and faster they danced, dipping and twirling like a pair of fancy ballroom professionals. Suddenly Stitch whipped himself into a tight spin and went whizzing down the aisle like a tornado, headed straight for Mrs. Hasagawa. Before the old woman realized what hit her, she went flying through the air and landed in a pile of watermelons. She sat up with a watermelon on her head.

"Why is everything so dark?" she asked.

Next, Nani tried the local coffee shop. "I am all about coffee," she told Kiki, the shop owner.

Meanwhile, Lilo moved Stitch on to his next lesson. "Elvis played guitar," Lilo said. "Here." She handed Stitch a small ukulele. "Hold it like this. And put your fingers here. . . ." She strummed Stitch's paw across the strings.

"I make great cappuccinos and lattes—" Nani was saying when she was suddenly interrupted by an impressive ukulele solo. Nani and Kiki watched in astonishment as Stitch's claws flew faster and faster over the strings, until . . .

CRASH! All the windows in the coffee shop shattered. Kiki jumped as the coffeepot in her hand exploded, blown apart by the high-pitched wail coming from Stitch's ukulele.

Soon after that, Nani was standing before the reception desk in the lobby of a fancy hotel, trying to sweet-talk the manager into hiring her. "I just love to answer phones," she told him.

Lilo had decided that the hotel lobby was the perfect place to give Stitch a lesson in romance.

"This is the face of romance," Lilo told Stitch as she pointed at a picture of Elvis.

Together they sauntered toward an older woman who was sitting alone on a couch, quietly reading a magazine.

"She looks like she could use some loving," Lilo said.

As Lilo watched, Stitch climbed onto the couch with a rose in his hand and took the woman's hand. The woman looked up from her magazine in surprise.

"Now kiss her," Lilo urged.

At the front desk, Nani and the manager both jumped as the woman's horrified scream rang through the lobby. A second later Nani bolted out of the hotel, dragging Lilo and Stitch behind her.

"I'm sure Elvis had his bad days, too," Lilo told Stitch consolingly.

By the time they reached the lifeguard's stand at beach, Nani had almost given up hope of finding a job. But she tried one last time. "I'm all about saving people," she told the head lifeguard.

"Actually, I do think we have an opening," the lifeguard said.

"Really?" Nani was ecstatic. "Oh, that would

be so great. You have no idea how badly I need this job."

Down the beach, Stitch was getting ready to put everything he'd learned into practice. Wearing a big black pompadour wig and a flashy white sequined jumpsuit, he waddled along the sand, gripping his ukulele. He stopped in front of a crowd of sunbathers.

"Knock 'em dead!" Lilo told him.

Stitch slowly started to play the ukulele. Suddenly a crowd of tourists swarmed around him, blinding him with a barrage of camera flashes.

The camera flashes confused Stitch. His eyes started to spin. His lips curled back over his teeth.

"Don't crowd him!" Lilo cried, trying to push through the tourists. But it was too late. Stitch turned into a snarling beast. He ripped off his costume. Howling like a wolf, he grabbed a woman's camera and bit it to pieces.

"Hey! Cut it out!" another tourist yelled, blasting Stitch with a stream of water from a giant water gun. But the water only made Stitch madder. He grabbed the surprised tourist and hurled him across the sand.

The crowd panicked. They scrambled over one another, pushing and shoving to get away from this frightening monster. In their frenzy, they knocked over the lifeguard stand.

Within moments, Stitch, Lilo, Nani, and the lifeguard were the only ones left on the beach. The lifeguard looked at Nani and shook her head. Without a word, she turned and walked away.

Nani and Lilo hung their heads in disappointment. They walked away from Stitch and plopped down in the sand near the toppled lifeguard station. Stitch was still confused by what had just happened. Standing alone on the empty beach, he picked up his smashed ukulele.

Just then, David wandered over with a surfboard tucked under each arm. "Hey, Lilo. How's it, Nani?"

"We've been having a bad day," Lilo told him.

David looked at Nani's sad expression. "Hey," he said. "I might not be a doctor, but

I know that there's no better cure for a sour face than a couple of boards and some choice waves. What do you think?"

Lilo looked at Nani. Nani smiled.

"I think that's a great idea," Nani said.

CHAPTER 14

The turquoise water sparkled in the sunlight as Nani and David paddled their surfboards across the water. Sitting on the back of Nani's board, Stitch peered down into the ocean. Below him, a large brown turtle swam by peacefully.

Lilo and David caught the first wave. As Stitch watched, they balanced on the water and gracefully steered David's board along the crest of the wave. Stitch was amazed. In all his short life, he'd never seen anything so beautiful. He stood up on his hind feet and clapped his paws together.

From that point on, Stitch watched everyone closely, imitating everything they did. When Lilo and David built a sand castle on the beach, Stitch tried to make one, too. Later that afternoon, he dragged a surfboard over to Lilo and begged to go back out surfing.

Perched high in a nearby coconut tree, Jumba watched them through his quadnoculars. "Wait!" he exclaimed as Stitch, Nani, and Lilo headed back into the ocean. "Something is not right. 626 is returning willingly to water."

His protest was interrupted by an incoming call on Pleakley's intergalactic communicator. Pleakley answered it—and yelped in surprise. The Grand Councilwoman glared at him from the screen.

"Mr. Pleakley, you are overdue. I want a status report," she commanded.

"Uh . . . things are going well," he said nervously. "Jumba, aren't they going well?"

But Jumba was busy watching Stitch. "He cannot swim!" he said to himself. "Why will he risk drowning?"

"Jumba, help me out here," Pleakley whispered.

"I would have expected you back by now with 626 in hand," the Grand Councilwoman said sternly.

Jumba reached over and switched off the

communicator. "Hang up," he said. "We are going swimming."

Out in the ocean, Stitch screamed with joy as he, Nani, and Lilo rode through the center of a curling wave. He was so happy, he didn't notice Jumba in the water behind him.

Roar! The wave crashed down on them as Jumba burst through the wall of water. He grabbed Stitch and pulled him under, knocking Lilo and Nani off the surfboard as well.

A few feet away, Nani and Lilo bobbed to the surface.

"What happened?" Lilo asked.

"Some lolo must have stuffed us in a barrel," Nani said, looking at the broken pieces of her surfboard.

Lilo looked around with concern. "Where's Stitch?" she asked. Just then Stitch popped up, gasping and splashing frantically. He grabbed Lilo just as Jumba pulled him under again. Before Nani could stop Stitch, he pulled Lilo down under the water with him.

David quickly swam over to help. "What happened?" he asked anxiously.

"Stitch dragged her down!" Nani cried. Quickly they both dove underwater. Nani grabbed Lilo and pulled her away from Stitch. A second later, Nani, David, and Lilo burst to the surface, gasping for air.

"We lost Stitch!" Lilo cried. David took a deep breath and dove back down.

Deep underwater, Stitch and Jumba wrestled with each other as Pleakley, wearing a mask and scuba tank, swam around them, trying to handcuff Stitch. But the aliens were no match for the little blue beast. Grabbing Pleakley, Stitch slammed him into Jumba's head, then handcuffed the two of them together. With his sharp teeth, Stitch bit down on Pleakley's scuba tank. A stream of pressurized air burst from the tank, launching Jumba and Pleakley out of the water like a torpedo.

Stitch tried to swim to the surface, but he'd run out of strength. The last thing he saw before he lost consciousness was David swimming toward him.

"Lilo, look at me, baby! Are you hurt?" Nani asked frantically as she dashed from the ocean with Lilo in her arms.

"No," Lilo answered.

A second later, David ran out of the water, holding a waterlogged Stitch. Lilo ran to meet them just as Stitch burst to life, scratching and clawing like a wild animal. Nani pulled Lilo out of his way just in time.

But their trouble wasn't over. At that moment, Nani noticed Cobra Bubbles standing nearby. He had seen everything.

Nani handed Lilo to David and rushed over to Cobra. "This isn't what it looks like," she said desperately. "We were . . . it's just that . . ." Nani tried to explain what had happened.

"I know you're trying, Nani, but you need to think about what's best for Lilo," he told her. "Even if it removes you from the picture." Nani looked down at the ground, unable to think of anything to say. "I'll be back tomorrow morning for Lilo. I'm sorry," Cobra added. Stung by his words, Nani watched speechlessly as he walked back to his car.

David walked up, carrying Lilo. "Is there something I can do?" he asked.

"No, David," Nani said as she took Lilo into her arms. I need to take Lilo home now. We have a lot to talk about, you know? Thanks." Then she gathered Lilo into her arms and slowly carried her away.

Stitch and David watched them go. "I really believed they had a chance," David told Stitch. "Then you came along."

Stitch's ears drooped in dismay. Suddenly he realized that he was to blame for all of Nani and Lilo's problems. And for the first time ever, Stitch felt . . . sad.

CHAPTER 15

As Stitch slowly climbed a series of wooden steps up the hillside above Lilo and Nani's house, he came upon a lone goose standing before him in the moonlight. The two of them stared at each other for a moment. Then the goose honked softly, summoning a group of tiny goslings. The scene reminded Stitch of Lilo's story about the ugly duckling.

Nani and Lilo sat in the hammock outside their house. Nani tried to tell Lilo that Cobra Bubbles was coming the next day to take Lilo away. "Lilo, we have to . . . ," Nani started.

Sensing Nani's anguish, Lilo said, "Don't worry . . . you're nice and someone will give you a job. I would."

Nani sighed and held out her arms invitingly. "Come here." Nani softly sang a beautiful Hawaiian song to Lilo. She knew she needed to tell Lilo they couldn't live together anymore, but she couldn't bring herself to do it. Not just yet.

Stitch watched them from the shadows at the edge of the porch as Nani pulled out the flowers that Lilo had in her hair. The flowers blew away into the warm night.

Later that evening in Lilo's room, Stitch lifted the pillow on Lilo's bed. He looked at the photograph she kept hidden beneath it. It was a picture of Lilo, Nani, and their parents, laughing happily together.

"That's us before," Lilo told him. She looked at the picture of her parents. "It was rainy and they went for a drive. What happened to yours?" She looked at Stitch. "I hear you cry at night. Do you dream about them?"

Stitch's ears lifted in surprise. He didn't know how to answer her. He climbed down off Lilo's bed and shuffled over to his pineapple-crate bed.

"Our family's little now, and we don't have many toys," Lilo told him. "But if you want, you could be part of it. You could be our baby and we'd raise you to be good."

Stitch reached into his crate and pulled out *The Ugly Duckling.* Tucking the book under his arm, he walked over to the window and climbed up on the sill. Lilo lowered her head sadly. She looked at him out of the corner of her eye.

"*'Ohana* means family. Family means nobody gets left behind, but if you want to leave you can," she told him. Stitch hesitated for a moment. Then he climbed out the window.

"I'll remember you, though," Lilo said as he left. She looked again at the photo of her family, then slid it back under her pillow. "I remember everyone that leaves."

As Lilo put her head on the pillow and fell asleep, Stitch peered through the window one last time. Then he was gone.

Stitch walked deep into the forest, carrying the storybook under his arm. At last he came to a clearing. The moon shone down through the trees, bathing the ground in silver light.

Stitch sat down in the moonlight and opened his book. He looked at the picture of the sad, lonely little duckling.

"Los—los—" he stammered. "Lost." Stitch lifted his head and cried up to the sky, "I'M LOST!"

But no one came.

Miles away, on another part of the island, Jumba and Pleakley were lying on a rocky reef, trying to catch their breath. They were battered and bruised from their underwater battle with Stitch and their unexpected scuba-tank-powered flight.

Suddenly Pleakley's intergalactic communicator rang. The Grand Councilwoman's face blinked onto the monitor. She was furious that they still hadn't caught 626.

"Consider yourselves fired and prison-bound," she told them. "Your incompetence is nothing short of unspeakable." Then she hung up. The screen went blank.

"We're fired," Jumba said. Pleakley turned

pale and started to cry.

But Jumba was smiling. "Now we do it my way!" he announced. He stormed off through the bushes.

"Your way?" said Pleakley. "No, wait!" He jumped to his feet and chased after Jumba.

CHAPTER 16

The early-morning sun peeped through the trees of the quiet forest, shining softly on the bushes and flowers. On the forest floor, Stitch lay fast asleep, clutching his book.

A nearby bush rustled. The sound woke Stitch. He sat up and looked eagerly around. His ears lifted hopefully. Had his family finally come to get him?

But it wasn't Stitch's family that came out of the bushes. It was Jumba! Stitch watched as the giant purple alien crept toward him.

"Don't run!" Jumba said. "Don't make me shoot you. You were expensive. Now come quietly."

Stitch shook his head and stayed put. "Waiting," he told Jumba.

"For what?" Jumba asked. Just then Jumba's

foot fell on Stitch's book. He looked at it curiously.

"Family," said Stitch.

Jumba stared at him in amazement. "You don't have one. I made you."

"Maybe I could—" Stitch started to say. But Jumba cut him off.

"You're built to destroy," he told the little blue creature. "You can never belong."

Stitch was crushed. All he'd wanted was to find his family, just like the ugly duckling. But he didn't have a family.

Jumba moved toward him. "Now come quietly," he said.

Stitch paused for a moment; then he dashed off through the trees.

Back at the house, Nani was slumped over a cup of coffee at the kitchen table. She'd been up crying most of the night. She glanced over at the clock, knowing it was only a matter of time before Cobra Bubbles came to take Lilo away.

Lilo quietly came into the kitchen. "Lilo,

what's wrong?" Nani asked, seeing her sister's drooping shoulders.

Lilo shrugged. "Stitch left." She turned her face away so Nani wouldn't see how sad she felt. "It's good he's gone," she said, trying to convince herself she meant it. "He didn't want to be here anyway. We don't need him."

Nani sighed and pulled her sister close. She knew she couldn't put off telling Lilo the truth any longer. "Lilo," she began, "sometimes you try your hardest but things don't work out the way you want them to. Sometimes things have to change, and maybe sometimes they're for the better... even if—"

Bang, bang, bang! Nani was interrupted by a knock at the door. Her heart sank. She went to the door and opened it to see ...

"David?"

David was grinning from ear to ear. "I think I found you a job at Old Man Kalakini's store!" he said. "But we gotta hurry!"

Nani's spirits suddenly surged. This could make all the difference! If she had a job, maybe Cobra wouldn't take Lilo after all. She rushed over to her little sister. "Lilo, baby, this is really important. I need you to stay here for a few minutes. I'm gonna be right back. Lock the door and don't answer it for *anyone*. Okay?" She kissed Lilo and ran out with David.

CHAPTER 17

Moments after Nani left, Lilo heard the dog door swing open and closed. Had Stitch come back? She hurried to see.

"Stitch?" she called out. Suddenly Stitch grabbed her hand. He put his claw to his lips and whispered, "Shhh!"

A loud crash came from the room next to them. Lilo jumped. Someone was in the house! Suddenly a giant purple alien rounded the corner and charged straight at them!

"Ha, ha!" Jumba boomed when he saw Stitch. "Hiding behind your little friend won't help anymore. Didn't I tell you? We got fired this morning. New rules." He aimed his plasma cannon right at Lilo and Stitch and squeezed the trigger.

Stitch threw Lilo out of the way. Quick as

lightning, he reached out and caught the bolt of molten plasma.

"Ow, ow, ow!" Stitch cried, tossing the scorching plasma in his hands. He took aim and hurled the plasma ball at Jumba's head, knocking him backward. As Jumba stumbled to his feet, Stitch escaped down the hallway.

Jumba crept after him, peering into every room. "Come out, my friend, from whomever you are hiding behind," he called. A small movement suddenly caught his attention. It was Lilo's doll, Scrump, strapped to a squeaky roller skate. Jumba leaned in for a closer look and . . .

BOOM! Scrump exploded, sending Jumba flying into the kitchen. When the dust cleared, Jumba spotted Stitch, scuttling across the ceiling like a fly. "Come on! What's the big deal?" he asked.

"Inga tu smishta!" Stitch cried.

"I'll put you back together again," Jumba promised as he hurled plates at Stitch. The plates shattered against the ceiling. "I'll make you taller . . . and not so fluffy!"

"I *like* fluffy!" Stitch replied. Just then, the

ceiling caved in. Stitch tumbled to the floor and was buried under a heap of plaster and wood. Jumba aimed his cannon at the pile of rubble.

"No!" Lilo cried. She whacked Jumba with a broom. Jumba looked over at her. Suddenly Stitch burst out of the rubble and hurled Jumba against the wall.

Lilo grabbed Stitch's hand and led him to the back door. "Quick! Follow me!" she cried. She threw open the door and saw . . . a skinny green alien with one giant eye in the middle of his face.

Pleakley was overjoyed to see Lilo. "You're alive!" he cried.

"They're all over the place!" Lilo screamed and slammed the door in Pleakley's face.

Jumba appeared behind them, blocking their escape. There was no way out. "Running away?" he said. "Here, let me stop you!"

At that moment, Jumba hurled a giant knife-like object toward the door. Pleakley swung the door open again, pushing Lilo and Stitch aside. Seeing that the sharp object was heading straight for him, Pleakley quickly slammed the door shut again. Fortunately, the door stopped the weapon just an inch or two from Pleakley's stomach.

"You always get in the way!" Jumba growled at him. Pleakley followed Jumba into the house.

"Where's the girl?" Pleakley cried. "What have you done to the girl?"

Meanwhile, Lilo had made her way to the phone and dialed the number on the card Cobra had given her. "Hello, Cobra Bubbles?" she shouted. "Aliens are attacking my house!"

Pleakley rushed to stop her. "No! No! No!" he cried. "No aliens!"

A loud rumble shook the house. Suddenly Stitch smashed through the kitchen wall with a car. Only he wasn't *driving* the car. He was *carrying* it!

Wham! Stitch swung the car like a baseball bat and knocked Jumba into Nani's bedroom.

Lilo was still shouting into the phone. "They want my dog!" she told Cobra.

"There is no need to alert the authorities," Pleakley pleaded. "Everything is under control!" he shouted into the telephone receiver.

Cobra Bubbles was listening closely on the other end of the line. "Lilo? Who was that?" he asked. He heard a loud buzzing in the background.

"Oh, good," Lilo told him. "My dog found the chain saw." Before Cobra could say another word, Lilo had hung up the phone.

Meanwhile, Stitch had launched himself off the trunk of the car and was flying through the air with the chain saw. "Heeheehee!" he cackled, enjoying himself thoroughly.

Jumba grabbed the only thing he could find—a toilet plunger—and hurled it at Stitch. The plunger landed right on Stitch's head, causing him to drop the chain saw.

Just as Jumba was about to pull the plasma cannon's trigger, Stitch grabbed a carrot and stuck it into the cannon's barrel. Realizing that the clogged cannon was going to explode, Jumba smiled and threw it to Stitch. Stitch grinned and threw it back at Jumba. Pleakley grabbed Lilo, slung her over his shoulder, and ran from the house.

Back and forth Jumba and Stitch threw the

plasma cannon as if it were a hot potato. "One potato . . . two potato . . . three potato, four," they called. When the game ended, Jumba ended up holding the plasma cannon. At first he was pleased. "Ha! I win," he said triumphantly. Then he realized what was about to happen—

KABOOOOM! Lilo's house exploded in a ball of fire.

CHAPTER 18

By the time Nani returned home, Cobra Bubbles was already standing outside the smoldering house with Lilo. When he saw Nani, Cobra immediately ushered Lilo into his car and closed the door. Lilo watched through the car window as Nani and Cobra spoke.

"Please don't do this," Nani begged.

"You know I have no choice," answered Cobra.

"No!" Nani shouted. "You're not taking her!"

"You're making this harder than it needs to be," Cobra told her sternly.

"You don't know what you're doing! She needs me!" Nani pleaded.

"Is *this* what she needs?" Cobra pointed to the remains of their house. Nani's mouth opened and closed soundlessly. "It seems clear to me that you need her a lot more than she needs you."

Behind Cobra's back, the door of the car cracked open. Neither Nani nor Cobra noticed as Lilo silently slipped out of the car and ran into the forest.

Lilo didn't know where she was going. She only knew she wanted to get away from there. She dashed through the bushes, ignoring Nani's and Cobra's calls for her.

Suddenly Stitch popped out from the bushes right in front of Lilo.

"Ahhhh!" Lilo screamed in surprise.

Stitch silently held something out to Lilo. It was the photo of her family. He'd found it in the smoking rubble of the house.

Lilo's eyes opened wide at the sight of the burned photo. The last evidence of her family had been destroyed.

"You ruined everything!" she cried.

Stitch took a breath, stretched his arms, and transformed back into his alien shape. Lilo stared. "You're one of them?" she asked in horror.

Stitch nodded sheepishly. Lilo shoved him, hard. "GET OUT OF HERE, STITCH!" she shouted.

But before Stitch could move, a net flew over both him and Lilo, tangling them into a ball. A massive figure stepped out of the bushes. It was Captain Gantu! On the Grand Councilwoman's orders, he'd come to Earth to get Stitch himself.

"Surprise! And here I thought you'd be difficult to catch." Gantu chuckled. "Silly me." Gantu scooped up Lilo and Stitch and carried them through the woods to his spaceship.

CHAPTER 19

"**L**ilo?" Nani called. She walked farther and farther into the forest, hoping for some sign of her sister.

Suddenly Nani was knocked to the ground as something enormous pushed past her. Looking up, she saw Captain Gantu's giant legs crashing through the trees toward his spaceship. And he was carrying Lilo!

Nani watched in horror as Gantu dumped Lilo and Stitch into a bubble-like containment pod, then attached the pod to the back of his ship.

"There you go." He sneered at Stitch. "All buckled up for the trip. And look." He pointed to Lilo. "I even caught you a little snack."

Gantu climbed into the cockpit and started up the engines.

"No! Stop!" Nani cried, racing toward the spaceship. But she was too late.

As the ship lifted off, Stitch wriggled out of the containment pod and tumbled to the ground. Gantu's ship soared into the sky, with Lilo still trapped inside.

Stitch stumbled out of the bushes, rubbing his sore head where it had hit the ground. And then—*wham!* Nani whacked him over the head with a tree branch.

"Okay, I know you had something to do with this. Now, where's Lilo? *Talk!*" she demanded. "I know you can."

Stitch sighed. "Okay, okay," he said. Nani screamed in fright and hit him on the side of the head again. It wasn't every day that she saw a talking alien.

But before Stitch could say another word, he was suddenly blown off his feet by a blast from a plasma cannon. Jumba dove from the bushes, tackled Stitch, and locked him in handcuffs. Then he slammed Stitch against a palm tree again and again. Stitch squeaked with every swing.

Pleakley was pleased they had finally caught Stitch. "You're under arrest!" he said. "Read him his rights." Then Pleakley called the Grand Councilwoman to tell her the good news.

Gathering all her courage, Nani stepped forward.

"Don't interact with her," Pleakley said quietly to Jumba.

Jumba and Pleakley turned their backs, pretending not to notice her.

"Where's Lilo?" Nani asked the aliens.

"Who?" Jumba responded, forgetting what Pleakley had just told him.

Nani stepped even closer. "Lilo. My sister," she said. She looked at them pleadingly.

"Uh . . . sorry. We do not know anyone by this name," Jumba said unconvincingly.

"*Lilo!*" Nani shouted. "She's my *sister*! She's a little girl. She has black hair and brown eyes and she hangs around with that *thing*!" She blinked back angry tears. "You know her. You have to!"

"We know her," Jumba said.

"Bring her back," Nani demanded.

"Oh, we can't do that!" Pleakley objected. "That would be misuse of galactic resources." Jumba put a hand on Pleakley's chest and pushed him aside.

"See, problem is, we're just here for him," Jumba explained. He pointed to Stitch.

"So she's gone. . . ." Nani sank to the ground in shock.

"Look at the bright side," said Pleakley. "You won't have to yell at anyone anymore."

Nani put her face in her hands and sobbed.

Jumba turned to Stitch. "Come," he said. Jumba, Pleakley, and Stitch slowly walked away.

But Stitch stopped. Something occurred to him and he walked back to where Nani was kneeling. "*Ohana,*" he said.

Nani looked up. "Huh?"

"Hey, get away from her!" Jumba shouted, trying to grab the handcuffed Stitch. But Nani pushed Jumba away. "What did you say?" she asked Stitch.

"*Ohana* means family," Stitch told her. "Family means . . ."

". . . nobody gets left behind," Nani finished.

"Or forgotten. Yeah," Stitch added. He turned to Jumba. "Hey! *Gambooka gabbly!*"

Jumba's face flushed with anger. *"What?"* he roared. "After all you put me through, you expect me to help you? *Just like that?"*

"Ih!" said Stitch.

"Fine!" Jumba agreed, to everyone's amazement. He reached down and unlocked Stitch's handcuffs.

"You're doing what he says?" Pleakley asked in total shock.

"He is very persuasive," Jumba explained.

"Persuasive?" Pleakley looked panicked. "What exactly are we doing?"

"Rescue," Jumba said.

"We're gonna get Lilo?" Nani leaped to her feet.

"Ih!" said Stitch.

Moments later, Stitch, Jumba, Nani, and Pleakley were roaring down the highway on a stolen motorcycle. As Jumba steered, Stitch sat on the handlebars, wearing a mischievous grin.

"Oh, good." Pleakley moaned. "I was hoping to add theft, endangerment, and insanity to my list of things I did today."

Jumba glanced back at him in surprise. "You too?"

Stitch giggled gleefully as the motorcycle turned onto a dirt road that led into the Hawaiian forest. When the road ended, the group abandoned the bike and hiked deeper into the trees until they came to a giant mound of vegetation. Jumba pulled a handful of palm leaves away from the pile, revealing the shiny red side of his spaceship.

Stitch's face lit up. A real spaceship! Now they were getting somewhere.

Jumba chuckled when he saw Stitch's excitement. "What?" he asked. "Did you think we walked here?"

Meanwhile, Captain Gantu's ship was soaring through the clouds.

"Requesting hyperspace clearance," he asked over the airwaves. But he was told to wait a minute before engaging his hyperspace drive.

At the back of his ship, Lilo sat alone in the containment pod. She glanced at the photo of her family and began to cry softly. She didn't think she would ever be rescued.

All of a sudden, a gleaming red shark fin–like wing pierced through the clouds. From the red ship's cockpit window, Stitch gave a friendly wave to Lilo. He had come to rescue her!

Back in Gantu's cockpit, an announcement came over the speaker system: "Hyperspace clearance granted on vector C12." Thinking he'd completed his mission, Gantu picked up his radio and called Galactic Headquarters.

"Gantu? Where are you? What's going on?" the Grand Councilwoman barked over the speaker.

Gantu smiled smugly. "I thought you'd like to know that the little abomination is . . . is . . . *Aah!*"

Gantu yelled in surprise as Jumba's giant spacecraft pulled up alongside his tiny ship. Standing in the cockpit window, Stitch wiggled his rear end tauntingly at the captain.

"Yes, Captain?" the Grand Councilwoman asked.

Just then, Jumba's ship rolled sideways, smacking the captain's ship with its giant wing. "I'll call you back," Gantu muttered. He hurriedly hung up the radio and scrambled to regain control of his spaceship.

A second later, Jumba's spacecraft burst out of the clouds, with Gantu hot on its trail. The larger ship zigzagged through the sky, dodging the blasts Gantu fired from his laser cannons.

Inside the ship, Jumba sat in the pilot's seat with Stitch at his side. Together they frantically worked the control panel.

Nani watched them nervously. "So what exactly are we doing?" she asked.

"Don't worry, is all part of plan," Jumba told her. "We are professionals."

By way of agreement, Stitch popped a control knob into his mouth and gnawed on it.

"Hey!" Jumba frowned. "Get that out of your mouth."

All of a sudden, a blast from Gantu's cannon

tore through the rear part of Jumba's ship. Pleakley screamed. The ship plummeted toward a jagged cliff on the island's coastline.

"Hold on!" Jumba shouted. He cranked the steering column and the huge ship rolled sideways, just squeezing through a narrow canyon between two towering cliffs.

Gantu's ship swerved downward and shot along a parallel canyon. Gantu growled in frustration as his ship glanced off the canyon's rock wall

"Okay, it's show time!" Jumba cried. Stitch hurried over to the spaceship's door and gripped the handle, a huge grin spreading across his face. Nani screamed and grabbed onto her seat for dear life. "This is it!" Jumba roared. With a twist of the steering column, he swerved the ship around a rock formation—smack into Gantu's ship! The smaller spacecraft flew out of control.

At that moment Stitch burst out the door and plunged through the air, giggling wildly. *Slam!* Stitch landed right on Gantu's windshield. The captain jumped back in surprise.

Stitch scurried over the top of Gantu's ship to the containment pod where Lilo was trapped. Lilo's face lit up with joy as Stitch began to claw his way into the pod.

"Little savage! Get off my ship!" Gantu growled when he saw what Stitch was doing. He pulled a lever to engage the transport's rear engines, blasting Stitch off the back of the speeding ship.

Through the floor of the containment pod, Lilo watched with horror as Stitch plummeted to the earth, miles and miles below.

CHAPTER 20

Wham! Stitch slammed into the ground. He bounced from hilltop to hilltop before finally sliding to a stop in the middle of a road. A fat bullfrog stared at him. *"Ribbit!"*

High in the air above him, Gantu's spaceship computer had pinpointed Stitch's exact location. "We finish this now," Gantu growled. He veered away from Jumba's ship and zoomed toward the unconscious Stitch. Setting the sights of his laser cannons, Gantu fired.

Suddenly the bullfrog hopped onto Stitch's forehead. Stitch opened his eyes . . . and leaped out of the way just in the nick of time! The laser blast tore a hole in the ground next to him.

"No!" Gantu shrieked furiously. He spun the ship around to re-aim at Stitch. As he did, Lilo's pod passed over Stitch's head.

"Don't leave me, okay?" Lilo begged him through the glass.

Stitch's heart sank. "Okay . . . okay . . . ," he agreed, looking around desperately for a way to save her. Just then a truck horn blared behind him. Stitch turned to see a huge gasoline truck coming over the hill.

"Okay!" Stitch shouted happily as he grabbed hold of the truck's bumper and brought it to a halt. The driver's jaw dropped when he turned to see what had stopped him— a tiny alien holding the three-ton semi by its back bumper!

Honk, honk! The gasoline truck bounced over a field of lava rocks, with Stitch at the wheel. He could barely see over the dashboard as he steered the semi toward a pool of molten lava. Squealing with glee, Stitch crashed the truck into the bubbling pool. As the truck slowly sank into the lava, Stitch climbed onto the gasoline tank.

Gantu's ship streaked toward him, with its

cannons blazing. The blasts rained around Stitch, splattering lava into the air.

"Abomination," the captain growled.

"Stupid head," Stitch snapped back.

KABOOOM! The gasoline caught fire and exploded, hurling Stitch through the windshield of Gantu's ship. As the smoke cleared, Stitch shouted, *"Aloha!"* landing upright on the ship's dashboard.

"You!" Gantu spluttered. "You're vile, you're foul, you're . . . flawed!"

Stitch grabbed Gantu's collar. "Also cute and *fluffy,*" he said just before he hurled the captain out of the ship. Gantu flew through the air and landed on the wing of Jumba's ship. He whipped out his plasma cannon and began to shoot his own ship to pieces!

On board Gantu's transport, Stitch climbed across the outside of the flaming vessel to where Lilo was trapped. He smashed a hole through the pod with his head and scooped up Lilo.

"You came back," Lilo said happily.

"Nobody gets left behind," Stitch told her. Lilo kissed the little alien on his nose. Holding

Lilo tight, Stitch leaped into the air just as the ship exploded.

The blast rocked Jumba's spacecraft, knocking Gantu's plasma cannon from his hand. Watching the explosion from inside the ship, Nani gasped. "Lilo!" she cried in despair.

But suddenly, through the billowing black smoke, she spotted Lilo and Stitch, clinging to the side of Jumba's spaceship. They both held on to Captain Gantu.

"Good dog!" Lilo cheered.

Miles below in the Pacific Ocean, David was floating peacefully on his surfboard, enjoying the late-afternoon sun. He didn't notice the spaceship that flew out of the sky and landed in the water behind him. The ship skidded across the bay, creating a giant wave that washed over the unwary surfer.

When David surfaced, he saw a giant red spaceship floating next to him. Lilo, Stitch, Nani, and three strange-looking aliens were sitting on top of it.

"David!" cried Lilo.

"Hey, Lilo," David said.

"Can you give us a ride to shore?" Lilo asked.

David looked at the assorted creatures perched on the spaceship. "Uhhh . . . sure," he said. "But I'll have to make two trips."

"So you're from another planet," David said thoughtfully as he paddled Lilo and Stitch through the water. "How's the surfing there?"

When they reached the shore, Lilo's and David's eyes opened wide with surprise. The beach was covered with aliens! The huge Galactic Federation spaceship rested behind them on the sand.

Without warning, an armored hand reached out and plucked Stitch off David's board. "We have 626!" a Federation guard announced.

"Take him to my ship," said the Grand Councilwoman.

"Leave him alone!" Lilo cried. She ran toward Stitch. But before she could reach him, she was pulled back by a pair of strong arms.

"Hold on," Cobra Bubbles told her. Lilo stared. How did *he* get here? she wondered.

"Grand Councilwoman, let me explain," Captain Gantu started.

"Silence!" the councilwoman shouted. "I am retiring you, Captain Gantu."

Pleakley stepped forward. "Actually, credit for the capture . . ."

". . . goes to me," the councilwoman said severely. "You'll be lucky if you end up on a fluff trog farm after we sort this thing out."

"Er, I think I should be—" Jumba started to say. The Grand Councilwoman turned to him with a furious glare.

"You! You are the cause of all of this! If it wasn't for your Experiment 626, none of this—"

"Stitch," Stitch interrupted.

"What?" the Grand Councilwoman looked at him in surprise.

"My name, Stitch," he told her. "Does Stitch have to go in the ship?"

"Yes," said the astonished Grand Councilwoman.

"Can Stitch say good-bye?"

"Yes," she agreed, staring at him in wonder.

"Thank you." Stitch toddled over to Lilo and wrapped his arms around her. Lilo hugged him tightly.

"Who are you?" the Grand Councilwoman asked Lilo.

But Stitch answered for her. "This is my family," he explained. "I found it all on my own. It's little and broken, but it's still good." Stitch nodded. "Yeah, still good."

Pleakley swallowed hard. "Does he really have to go?" he asked.

"You know as well as I that our laws are absolute," said the Grand Councilwoman. "I cannot change what the council has decided."

Cobra Bubbles suddenly stepped forward. "Lilo, didn't you buy that thing at the shelter?"

"Hey!" Lilo's sad face suddenly lit up with a grin. She ran to the councilwoman. "Three days ago, I bought Stitch at the shelter. I paid two dollars for him. See this stamp?" She waved her pink license receipt in the air. "I own him. If you take him, you're stealing."

The Grand Councilwoman took the receipt

and examined it carefully. Maybe she could let Stitch stay on Earth.

"Aliens are all about rules," Cobra explained to Lilo.

The Grand Councilwoman peered at him. "You look familiar."

"CIA," Cobra told her. "Roswell, 1973."

"Ah, yes," said the Grand Councilwoman. "You had hair then." She turned to the aliens on the beach and announced her decision. "Take note of this," she declared. "This creature has been sentenced to life in exile, a sentence that shall be henceforth served out here on Earth. And as caretaker of the alien life form 'Stitch,' this family is now under the official protection of the United Galactic Federation." She turned to Cobra. "We'll be checking in now and then."

Cobra sighed. "I was afraid you were going to say that. This will not be easy to explain back at headquarters."

The Grand Councilwoman gave him a sympathetic look. "I know what you mean."

As the Grand Coucilwoman strode back to

her ship, she passed Jumba and Pleakley. "Don't let those two get on my ship," she muttered to one of her guards.

As the sun slowly set over the ocean, the Galactic Federation ship rose into the pink and orange clouds. Standing on the beach far below, Stitch and his new family waved good-bye.

Nani gaped at Cobra. "CIA?" she asked.

"Former," Cobra told her. "Saved the planet once—convinced an alien race that mosquitoes were an endangered species." He took off his sunglasses and looked Nani in the eye. "Now, about your house . . ."

CHAPTER 21

With David, Jumba, Pleakley, and Cobra helping out, Lilo and Nani's house was rebuilt in no time. The new house was even better than the old one, with a big glass dome on top where Stitch could stay and watch the stars. While everyone worked, Stitch sat at the top of the house, serenading them on his guitar. He always played Elvis tunes, of course.

Along with her new house, Lilo had a whole new family! They did all the things that families do—but with a Stitch-style twist. Stitch made paper bag lunches for Nani and Lilo and walked Lilo to the school bus, just like a regular family member. He even went to hula class with Lilo. But when he baked a cake for Lilo's birthday, it came out as big as the oven! When it was Stitch's turn to do the laundry, he could never resist playing superhero. He would put a towel around his neck like a cape. Then he would run around like he was flying.

Holidays were extra special now, too! On Halloween, Stitch used his laser cannon to carve a pumpkin. At Christmastime, Jumba gave Lilo her very own spaceship! Stitch and Lilo took turns zooming around in it.

David was part of the family, too. He took Lilo, Nani, and Stitch out on his surfboard whenever they had the chance. With Nani on David's shoulders and Lilo and Stitch on Nani's shoulders they could all ride together, which was just how Lilo liked it.

Cobra, Jumba, and Pleakley fit right in to Lilo's unique family. They celebrated every holiday together. As the months went by, there was one more change in Lilo's life. On the wall over her bed, the pictures of tourists were replaced by a new photo collection. There were pictures of Lilo and Stitch hula dancing, pictures of Nani, Lilo, David, and Stitch on vacation, pictures of Cobra, Jumba, and Pleakley at the beach, pictures of everyone at

Thanksgiving dinner. And next to them all was the burnt photo of Lilo with Nani, her parents . . . and Stitch. Lilo had pasted a photo of her little blue friend to the picture. Now she could look at her whole family. Together.

ALOHa!